I0538012

The Adventures of J. Jones

By. A.G. Fielder

THE ADVENTURES OF J. JONES

BLACK GOLD

A.G. FIELDER

This book is a work of fiction. Names, characters, places and incidents are the product of the imaginations of the authors or are used fictitiously. Any resemblance to actual events, locales, or persons, living or dead, is coincidental.

Copyright © 2012-2013 by A. G. Fielder/Angela G. Fielder
All rights reserved

Cover design by Kalina Sotirova.

No part of this book may be reproduced in any form or by any electronic or mechanical means including information storage and retrieval systems, without permission in writing from the publisher and the author; not the contributor. The only exception is by a reviewer, who may quote short excerpts in a review.

Visit my website at www.agfielder.net
Contact the cover designer Kalina Sotirova at sotirka@gmail.com

Printed in the United States of America
Second Printing: May 2013

Labyrinth Press
PO Box 8061
Elkridge, MD 21075

ISBN-13: 978-0615824802
ISBN-10: 0615824803
BISAC: Fiction/Espionage

Acknowledgements:

Special thanks to Clinton H. Wallace who served as an advisor with select contributions on this particular installment of the series. Thank you for the advice and long talks.

Author's Note:

To Elijah, Mommy loves you always.

Illustrations by Alfonso Rosso

The Adventures Of J. Jones

Black Gold

Redux

By: A.G. Fielder

Labyrinth Press

Prologue

Ramadan, 2010
Arabian Desert

Hot arid winds of the Persian Gulf blew swiftly across the golden sands of the Arabian Desert. The wind-carved sand dunes and rugged wadis bore silent witness to muffled shots resonating from a secret enclave in the dry valley. In the flames of war, nothing is sacred. Two men wearing the immaculately pressed gleaming white dishdasha, gafia and gutra native to the Arabian Peninsula emerged from the enclave and walked back to the white Land Rover LR4 that was parked nearby. A satellite telephone rang not once but twice which jolted the gagged and tied up man in the trunk of the SUV. His eyes darted nervously around the trunk compartment as beads of sweat streamed down his bruised face. The desert heat was stifling and the man couldn't help but wonder if death would be a more accommodating companion as opposed to life encapsulated in the dense, humidity of the trunk. He knew he'd betrayed them, but never figured on them discovering the truth. A western man in the Arab world can often make careless mistakes that warrant cruel and unusual punishment. Arrogance is one such a mistake.

Straining to hear the conversation from the phone call, the man struggled to quiet his thoughts. The voices spoke in muffled Arabic. Heaving as he inhaled what little oxygen was left in the back of the SUV, the man listened to all of the details being discussed just outside the vehicle. Sweat from his brow burned his green eyes as he tried to steady his breath hearing just what he needed to in order to plot his next move.

"It is finished!" said one of the men in Arabic. "*Naam*," he continued as the man in the trunk did his best to translate what he was hearing. He could tell that the men were Pakistani by the cadence of their speech. To his chagrin, it was clear that his time had come.

"And what of the other?" the man continued. The bound man in the trunk squirmed in panic after the Pakistani man paused a beat before answering.

"*Mish mushkila*. It shall be done" the rogue Pakistani man said finally. As he ended the call he told his confidante to dispose of the other body and meet him in the rear of the SUV. Banging his left fist twice against the car door, the man taunted the victim, enjoying the stench of western fear like a tiger does blood. Rounding the back of the truck he opened the trunk door and hissed venomous words to his prisoner.

"Westerner...in your country you say it is better to beg for forgiveness than to ask for it, no?" he asked rhetorically. Drawing his snub-nosed, Slovak, K100 pistol and sliding it down the victim's sand-scuffed face, his white teeth gleamed in the blinding desert sun as the bound man began to tremble in shock.

"So beg!" he demanded stoically snickering in that deep throaty laugh that signaled danger on the horizon.

Snatching back his gun the Pakistani man shut the door abruptly and made his way over to the wadi.

For the first time, fear engulfed the westerner as he struggled with hands bound tightly behind his back to press the panic button installed on his watch. He had doubts that the signal could be sent from this far out in the desert.

His mind began to wander after he managed to press the button with the ring finger of his right hand. Like the desert sands, time was drifting and his was sure to come to an end soon. He wondered how long it would be before his tormentors returned and sent him to the crossroads of life and death. Closing his eyes he tried desperately to let his soul return to better days in the States and what he would've done before that fateful meeting on the cocktail circuit in the District that led him to where he was right now. Sadly, he thought that even if he could turn back the hands of time, he may have somehow still chosen a road that led him down the same path.

Footsteps in the sand are usually silent, but somehow he could feel them coming closer. With staggered breaths he whispered a prayer allowing the words "El Shaddai" to linger upon his dry, chapped lips. As fear set in deeper, a tear glided down the left side of his cheek. The end was unmistakably near. With eyes asquint the prisoner took several breaths as the door to the trunk once again opened.

"I will ask you once more," began one of the men, with gun in hand. "Are you one of their assets?"

"On my life, Masood, I do not know what you're talking about," the bound man said through the rag he was gagged by, his voice trembling in fear.

"Secrets and lies are what you westerners are full of," Masood continued as he cocked the gun and placed it against the man's chest. "I know you infiltrated the Libyan economy and helped the regime hide the money at Calvary Ltd."

"Masood, I...I..." he pleaded as a single shot resonated in the desert wind.

"May Allah have mercy on your soul," Masood said as the blood of the westerner began to pour out of the trunk door into the desert sand. He shut the door abruptly before placing his gun back in his holster and making his way over to his colleague at the wadi.

A military Super Puma chopper blazed off of the launch pad of the Burj-al-Arab Hotel in Dubai. The pilot, debriefed Agent Jones on how a distress signal was received at the base in Abu Dhabi and he was told to accommodate the federal agent in any way possible. Jones was to retrieve the western asset held captive and take him - or what was left of him - to the safe house for interrogation. The only problem was that time was not on their side.

"How much longer?" Jones asked.

"2 minutes."

"We don't have that much time!" Jones grumbled scanning the chopper for landing gear.

"Parachutes and wind suits are behind your seat, sir." the pilot began. "Entering prevailing winds...15 knots."

"Shit!" Jones said, unbuckling his seatbelt, he quickly put on the wind suit and secured it to his body.

"Agent Jones, I see the target. The signal is coming from the trunk of the SUV."

"I need eyes" Jones demanded just as he lowered his binocular goggles over his eyes. "Nevermind!"

"Sir, I will hover."

"No need. I'm going in. There are two targets, when you see them, proceed with annihilation."

"Yes sir."

As the helicopter hovered in the back of the enclave, the two Pakistani men who were busy disposing of the body, quickly dropped it, retrieved their guns and began shooting up at the helicopter which shot back nearly missing one of the Pakistani men. Jones jumped out of the chopper in the wind suit which enabled him to land in the sand safely. Dusting himself off, he fumbled for his gun before making his way to the parked SUV.

Running through the sand, Jones thought he was too late, until he heard the raised voices of the mercenaries quickly drawing near. Without a second to waste, he managed to make it over to the SUV and just as he reached to open the door, gunshots grazed his wrist.

"You are too late," sneered one of the Pakistani men in a thick accent. "We have already disposed of the westerner."

"Not on my watch!" Jones barked back, drawing his gun while crouched at the driver's side of the SUV.

"Perhaps you will believe when you suffer a similar fate!" Shots were fired once again by the mercenaries below who were determined to kill Jones and destroy the chopper which was now hovering above the situation. Every time the pilot had one of the men in his crosshairs, Jones would block the shot.

"What is he doing?" the pilot barked. Meanwhile, in the sand, Jones was still dodging bullets from the gunmen.

"You do not realize what you have done, Agent Jones!" yelled one of the gunmen.

"On the contrary! It is you who doesn't realize what you've gotten yourself into!" Jones said giving the silent signal to the pilot to take the final deadly shot.

Caught in the crosshairs, four shots were fired from the chopper that immobilized one of the Pakistani men, as the other man, now wounded, started running back towards the wadi to hide. As the chopper followed the man, Jones dashed to the back of the SUV and opened the door to find his asset shot in the chest with a faint pulse. Pressing the button on his watch he yelled,

    "He's alive!"

    "Sending a medic to your location, Agent Jones" said a sultry, female voice over the speaker on his Patek Philippe watch.

.

"Everyone has an agenda. What's yours?"

-Dawud El-Hashem

1

Abu Dhabi Military Base
U.S. Operations Wing
Abu Dhabi, UAE

The sweltering sun of the Abu Dhabi desert was not something that Jones was looking forward to. Sunglasses and smiles greeted him, in spite of it all, as he descended out of the military chopper. From the look on the senior officer Cunningham's face he knew that things were not going to be good. Cunningham was never good at hiding things.

"Assalaam Alaikum, Mr. Jones," said an exotic, modestly dressed, Middle Eastern woman. While her hair was covered, her enchanting, kohl-rimmed, deep topaz eyes stunned him momentarily into nearly forgetting that he was at work.

"Wa Alaikum Assalaam, Miss..." But before he could get her name Cunningham interrupted.

"Jones, I see you've met Izzie!" Noticing their gaze, Cunningham quickly dismissed the woman and ushered Jones into the door of a nearby building and into the first office on the left.

"Izzie?" Jones pressed.

"Uhm-hmm. Ishtar al-Musabi. She's one of the senior analysts here on base. Born in Dubai educated in the States. Everyone calls her Izzie."

"Where'd she go to school?" Jones asked curiously.

"Stanford."

"Whoa!"

"Yeah. Smart girl."

"And beautiful.."

"Uhm-hmm. But enough about her. What happened out there with the asset - what's his name?"

Flipping through a pile of papers on a clipboard, Cunningham searched for the name of the asset.

"Don't know?"
"What d'ya mean you don't know? He was *your* asset."

"I mean, I don't remember. I was supposed to meet up with him for drinks later. He tweeted me twice with the hashtag #gotdemdeets. It was one of our secret meeting codes."

"You tweeted meeting codes?" Cunningham asked condescendingly.

"Yes, sir we did."

"Pretty stupid, dontcha think? I mean, did you actually think that the intel wouldn't be compromised through tweets. C'mon Jones. The Emirati aren't stupid people."

"So, I see."

"What else?"

Jones waited a beat before pulling out his iPhone from his right pants pocket.

"I got a few texts from him...yesterday...see?"

"You texted him too? This just keeps getting better," Cunningham sneered. "Whatever happened to face-to-face meetings?"

"It's technology, man! You know how it goes." Jones said lightly as Cunningham read through the texts. Glancing up from the iPhone, Cunningham shook his head before giving the phone back to Jones."

"I'm not getting anything from this," he said finally before walking over behind the desk and sitting down.

"We've got a real problem, Jones."

"Sir?" Jones said bewildered.

"The way I see it is that your asset was playin' you, and has been for months. He was supposed to get you the names of the Libyan officials who invested in transcontinental oil deals under the table with that investment company, Calvary Ltd. But he didn't , did he?"

"No, but I almost got that intel. I was going to get it tonight."

"Well Jones," Cunningham continued reaching for his cigar box, pulling one out, lighting it, and taking a puff. "Almost doesn't count. Calvary is allegedly based in the UK is that right?"

"Yes."

"But we have assets who have disclosed that Calvary's true headquarters are in Dubai. We already know how Libya helped with the infrastructure in Dubai but we need the names. Who was in bed with whom and is Calvary Ltd. washing money for Libya and other countries in the Arab world. Who's fooling who?"

Jones sat quietly wondering how in the hell he would get the answers to those questions. With two of his assets face down in the sand, he'd have to start calling in a few favors from international friends - something he didn't want to do. Before Cunningham could get in another word the phone rang in his office. The call ended as quickly as it began with Cunningham simply grunting once in approval prior to hanging up.

"Looks like you're shipping out!" he said just after placing the phone in the cradle.

"Shipping out?"

"Yup."

"To where?"

"Tripoli. You leave in an hour," Cunningham said putting out the cigar. There was a soft knock on the door which opened shortly thereafter to reveal Ishtar carrying a large, manila envelope. She gracefully handed it to Cunningham.

"Thank you." He said abruptly as he opened the envelope and handed the contents to Jones. Looking at the Libyan visa and passport Jones exhaled abruptly.

"I'm leaving now?"

"Yup."

"And my cover is an oilman? C'mon man! You couldn't get me a better cover than that?"

"Trust me Jones, it's the best we could do considering the timing. Besides, you'll fit right in! A chopper will take you to Dubai International and you'll fly into Tripoli on KLM. Upon landing look for a driver holding a sign that says Qadir."

"KLM?"Jones pressed.

"Yup. Problems?"

"Yes. They expect agents and assets to come in on KLM. Why not change it to Air India?"

"Air India... Point noted. Anything else?"

"Nah...that's it," Jones said rising from his seat and walking towards the door.

"Oh and Jones...this time get the intel!"

"Will do, Cunningham. Will do."

As Jones walked out Cunningham buzzed his secretary outside.

"You rang, sir?"

"Yes. Change that flight from KLM to Air India."

"Yes sir."

"And, get me a secure line to Tripoli 218-091-579-8812."

"Processing your request. One moment please....Now connecting your call, sir" said the secretary.

"Thank you."

It didn't take long for the call to go through. Ringing once, Cunningham was surprised at how quickly the call was answered by his Libyan asset.

"Agent Cunningham? To what do I owe the honor?" a British-accented male voice answered.

"Dawud El-Hashem...good to hear your voice as well!" Cunningham began with his normal sarcasm. "I'm sending one of my agents over to your neck of the woods and was hoping you could be of assistance, should he need it."

"But, of course! It is what the American government pays me for."

"Naturally."

"When will your agent... what's his name?"

"Jones. Jeronimo Jones!"

"Right! Agent Jones. When will he be arriving?"

"He'll be in Tripoli in about 5 hours."

"Excellent! Have you arranged for a driver, Cunningham?"

"That is why I called you Dawud."

"Ah... I see.! So I am to be Jones' personal chauffeur?"

"And handler!" Cunningham added.

"Great!" Dawud said condescendingly.

"I wouldn't have it any other way, my friend. Get at me when Jones touches down at T.I.P."

Will he be travelling alone?" Dawud pressed.

"Initially, yes and no."

"Does he know this?" Dawud asked noticing Cunningham's intentional silent response.

"Your silence speaks volumes, Agent Cunningham. So where is he to be transported?" Dawud continued.

"He's travelling under the name of Qadir. Arrangements have been made for him at the Radisson Blu. Everything will be in place by the time he gets there."

"Excellent. I will send a car for him," Dawud replied. "Anything else my friend?"

"That'll do it!"

As Cunningham ended the call he picked up a folder with photos of the two deceased assets talking with Jones at a cafe in Dubai. Shaking his head, he tossed the folder down on his desk and picked up the phone once more. Ringing his secretary once again he gave her detailed instructions.

"Call over to the embassy in Tripoli and request a visa for Izzie. Get a message to her. We're sending her out there to assist Jones on this one."

"Yes sir!" the secretary replied.

<u>2</u>

T.I.P. Airport
Ben Ghasir, Libya
34 Kilometers outside of Tripoli
8 hours later

The screech of wheels skidded as the Boeing 777 Air India plane landed on the black tarp of Tripoli International Airport. Known to the locals as T.I.P., it was one of the few airports that Jones was not entirely fond of. Truth is, Jones hated being in Libya. Sitting in his seat anxiously awaiting the captain's seatbelt sign to fade on, he tried to wrap his head around the reason that he was in Tripoli to begin with. Not that it wasn't a beautiful place to visit, it just wasn't a place he planned on being for business. At least not now with all of the political unrest.

Jones knew firsthand that Libya was a very dangerous location to do business and the dictator's iron grip kept the status quo in place. However, he had to get to the bottom of things. Jones was no stranger to the hot sands of Tripoli. A few years ago he managed to get into some heat over there. This time he only hoped he could surpass the sands of trouble by all means. He knew why Cunningham sent him to Tripoli. It was no secret. He was an accessible expert on all things Middle Eastern at Langley. He'd been groomed to work in the Muslim World from his many missions in Egypt, Lebanon, Syria, Bahrain and Kuwait. Jones understood very well the role that Middle Eastern puppet regimes played in the great western war game. He also knew that Libya, did not fall prey to the western puppet master and had refused to play ball with the iron-fisted European powers. The dictator of Libya would not bow to the west - unlike compadre figureheads of neighboring countries, he didn't care about visiting the White House and having his picture taken with an American president. He didn't need to. After all, the Libyan regime ruled from Africa's power seat -

sitting pretty on 47 billion barrels of priceless, black gold and making Libya the world's 9th largest oil reserve.

There was a certain amount of confidence that stayed with a man who knew that he had what the world wanted. There was a definitive pride that emanated from a man who was rumored in the West to piss oil and shit platinum bullions. Not to mention, there is an unequivocal arrogance that travels with a man who knows that he is the bridge between an African and Arab union that could prove to be the West's most formidable global financial adversary.

Jones reviewed the notes in his head until he knew them like he knew the back of his hand. Sitting stationary in the cabin of the plane as it was coming to a stop, he mulled over the situation a little bit more. Then all of a sudden, something clicked and everything began to make sense. The dictator had planned on using his country's wealth to usher in an African renaissance. Shaking his head slightly as he coyly stared out of the window, Jones thought it over a bit more. He knew too well that the Americans, the Brits and Western European powers would never let that happen. Putting all of that aside still didn't answer one lingering question - who got the Pakistanis involved? Not to mention how did the Pakistani hit men in the desert know his name?

The more he pondered, the more puzzled he became. Something about the whole Pakistani equation just didn't add up. Were they Pakistani Intelligence, Interpol or just rogues? Were they briefed on his arrival?

As the cabin of the plane finally cleared out, a beautiful Indian flight attendant gently reminded Jones that it was time to de-board. Smiling warmly, Jones thanked the lady, unfastened his seatbelt, gathered his black leather briefcase from the overhead compartment and walked out of the plane. Closing the cabin doors the Indian flight attendant entered the lavatory, peeled the black wig and prosthetic nose from her face, removed the dark contacts and pressed a single button on her cell phone. The phone hardly rang before it was answered.

"Cunningham? He's entering TIP," she said while simultaneously changing out of her clothes and slipping into a coral hijab.

"Perfect! Izzie, what is your location?"

"I am exiting the plane as we speak," she replied.

"Excellent. Once you get to the Radisson Blu you need to get to Room 432 - it's the room above his. Your reservation is under the name El-Hashem. Everything is awaiting your arrival."

"As in Dawud El-Hashem?"

"Yes."

"Do you know him or something?"

"Once upon a time, perhaps."

"Interesting."

"Indeed. Look, uh Cunningham, are the mics in place at the hotel?"

"Of course. But Izzie, I'm curious to learn of how you know Dawud."

"Agent Cunningham, with all due respect, I was born in the Arab World. Unlike Jones, I'm not just visiting."

"Are you implying that all Middle Eastern people know one another, because we both know that isn't true."

"Agent Cunningham, Dawud El-Hashem is a billionaire playboy with a portfolio that matches and surpasses the top five American billionaires on the Forbes 500. There aren't too many people on a global scale who aren't familiar with his name."

"Alright, Izzie. I see where you're going with this. Just make your way over to that hotel and make sure Jones doesn't see you."

"Copy that," she said stuffing the uniform into her backpack, ending the call and casually exiting the plane.

Meanwhile, as Jones stepped out of the boarding area and let his eyes take in the airport he remembered exactly why he hated TIP.

The airport in Tripoli can be pretty complicated. Everything and everyone is monitored. From this alone, Jones knew he had to keep a low profile. After all, he was simply here in Tripoli to follow his orders and scrounge up a few leads on how the Pakistani mercs were linked to Calvary Ltd. As he walked slowly through the terminal from his Air India flight, he calmly retrieved his British passport and searched frantically for the Libyan visa that Cunningham had given him. Tearing through his briefcase, he was sure that he had it with him. Unless, of course he'd placed it in his suitcase.

"Dammit!" he muttered as he calmly zipped up the front pocket of the briefcase. Oh well, he'd just have to wing it.

He remembered that this time his cover name was Daniel Qadir, and he was a British oilman on business in Tripoli. Closing his eyes briefly he quickly recalled the visa number that was issued. All he had to do was stay calm and request that they check his credentials against the visa number. While he knew that everything would check out, he wasn't entirely sure if the customs agent would be so accommodating. He took a deep breath and looked at the two people standing in front of him trying to keep a low profile.

Listening to the exchange the two people were having in Arabic with the customs agent, Jones wondered if he'd have to go through mountains of red tape like he did when last he was in Libya. Cunningham had reassured him with certainty that there'd be nothing to worry about, but still part of him wasn't entirely sure. He knew that by coming in on an Air India flight with a British passport he'd easily clear customs. It was a sure thing to do it this way. BP had their people in and out of Libya because they were in the process of negotiating for the drilling rights to thousands upon thousands of acres both onshore and offshore. BP was greedily trying to compete with the Algerians. As the next person in front of him presented the agents with the copy of the email that was sent, Jones snapped into his cover and feigned a proper British accent. He noticed how the two customs agents looked him over and began a quick exchange in Arabic before addressing him in English.

"Good Day, Mr..."

"The name is Qadir," Jones said in perfect Arabic with a British, Southern English, formal accent. He noticed the customs agent make eye contact with each other in astonishment and then with him briefly before going back to reviewing the passport.

"Your Arabic is good Mr. Qadir," began the agent to which Jones nodded smartly.

"Might I ask, if you are here on business or pleasure?"

"Business. I work with BP and am en route to the Ghadames basin," Jones continued now in English, his British accent unwavering.

"An oilman?"

"Yes." Jones replied noticing that no eyebrows were raised when he mentioned his destination. Westerners usually came in on Lufthansa or KLM but he figured that a British oilman coming in from Dubai on Air India would draw little scruntiny...and he was right.

"BP is one of the more respected Western companies here. Very well, then. Do you have your visa number, sir?"

"I seemed to have packed the email sent from the company in my suitcase. I do however, know the number," Jones offered as the Libyan customs agent again made eye contact with him.

"Not a problem, Mr. Qadir. I can bring it up here. I require your patience for one more minute, if you please," the customs officer said as he keyed in the information from the passport, pulled a scanned document from his printer and rummaged through the pile of visas. Within seconds he quickly stamped the visa and handed it with the passport back to Jones.

"Your visa is good for 45 days. I hope your stay proves fruitful. Welcome to Libya," the customs officer said.

"Inshallah!" Jones said graciously as he tucked the visa and passport in his briefcase, and cooly made his way past the customs area.

His plan worked like a charm and Jones smiled with relief as he exited the terminal, however the coast was not clear yet. Walking swiftly through the airport and to the carport outside, Jones kept a sharp eye on his surrounding as he glanced around for his contact. Almost immediately he spotted the sign that read "Qadir." He failed to notice Izzie in the coral hijab and sunglasses watching him from behind. She hailed a tazi and got in as Jones nodded to greet his driver, gave the man his luggage, and entered a separate car as the driver stashed the suitcase in the trunk of the black BMW 740 IL. The driver was supposed to shepherd him to the Radisson Blu, where he would check in and then meet a CIA asset and rep from Calvary Ltd., Dawud el-Hashem. Izzie knew this and was adamant about her driver moving fast. Lucky for her, Jones didn't see. Speeding off in the hot desert sun, Izzie glanced back at Jones noticing that he was in deep thought as he slid into the car.

He was thinking about how Cunningham told him during the briefing that the guy that the Pakistanistani mercenaries did in was also a rep from Calvary. Somehow he wasn't surprised.

"Mr. Qadir, we will be arriving at your destination in 20 minutes," said the driver in a smooth, bass-filled voice as he raised the dark glass partition that separated the driver from the passenger section. Jones nodded as he stared blankly out of the window.

Calvary Ltd was the kind of UK investment company that had their hands in all things Libya. It was an energy and infrastructure investment banking business. While Jones knew this he'd also heard rumors that Calvary was run by double and triple agents that were planning on selling the dictator and his secret African building plans out to the Europeans.

Jones had a feeling that the westerner that the Pakistanis killed - a white bred American by the name of Kyle Ribici - knew something or had some kind of access to clandestine intelligence that led to his suddendemise. Jones also knew that the second guy that the Pakistanis did in was a fellow agent who tried to get a vital asset out of Libya to a safe house in Abu Dhabi. Needless to say, it didn't happen. Somebody sold him out which is why the two were intercepted by the Pakistani mercs who were well trained in the art of blending in. They posed as Arabs so that when push came to shove, blame would be placed on the Arabs. That's where the blame was supposed to be placed, or was it to go on the dictator and his regime? Or the Algerians? Jones could not figure out the specifics.

Still staring out of the window, Jones continued to wonder about the murderous blame game? Who ordered the hit? Where did the Pakistanis come from and why? If the blame lay with the Algerians then he would know that the Brits were involved hence the Pakistanis. However if the blame went to the dictator then Jones would know that's where things got complicated because the hit could've been ordered by the Americans or the French. Either way Jones felt like it was a trap and he was being set up. He felt like he was walking on a tight rope where he was damned if he did and damned if he didn't and he didn't like it one bit. There were 30 days in the holy month of Ramadan and with the day nearly over, he knew that he didn't have much time to sort everything out without getting caught up. Whatever he did, he had to figure this out and quick, his life depended on it, and if things went awry he knew that there would be no hesitation by Cunningham and his Langley superiors to burn him. Times like this he wished he was sitting on his grandfather Percy's porch in DC, taking in the odd serenity of the quaint yet busy streets of DC's southeast side. But that serenity was a world away, so he glanced at the dark partition in front of him before his gaze returned to the signs of the freeway outside.

Karachi, Pakistanistan
Satellite Location of Calvary Ltd.
COO's Office
Same Day

It had just come to the attention of Mustafa Patel that a local journalist had divulged intimate and damaging details to WikiLeaks on the alleged, international conspiracy surrounding Calvary Ltd's secret oil investment deals with numerous political factions in the Arab world. Such revelations included the journalist validating public speculation on Patel's past noting that before he was COO and managing partner of Calvary, he had been a lieutenant during the early 1980s in what was then Pakistanistan's Genderarmes Special Ops Counterintelligence team - a strategic partner whose officers aligned themselves with America's calculus for global security. This was the very team that received American tactical CIA training in exchange for providing trade secrets on select Middle Eastern officials and the oil reserves that they owned at the time.

In Patel's mind, the only person who could have possibly leaked this information was a Dravidian reporter (born on the Arabian Peninsula) named Khalid Mutasi. Slamming his fists down on the desk, Patel wondered how he could've been so careless as to let Mutasi into his inner circle. At the time, it seemed like a good idea. After all, Mutasi, like he, had a life rooted in Islam. He was a man of Allah and worked for the better of pilgrims of the faith in Libya, Afghanistan, Sri Lanka, and his native Pakistanistan. Mutasi, after all, seemed to have a lot in common with Patel and was a businessman often doing business in both the Arab and Western worlds.

Patel felt upon meeting Mutasi that the man had no reason to lie about his work. Unfortunately Patel was dead wrong. Sitting behind his grand, mahogany desk, he listened in horror at what two agents from Pakistani intelligence were telling him. Mutasi had not only betrayed his trust and violated his company, he had also set Patel up for international conspiracy, racketeering and possible espionage charges in Pakistanistan, the U.K. and America. Such charges fell under what the west calls "money laundering". It had been noted that Mustafa Patel under the auspices of his company Calvary Ltd had not only washed millions of dollars for several hostile political regimes but the Pakistanistan and Dubai branches of Calvary had been blatantly accused of financing energy and illicit arms deals for these countries as well. Patel was outraged.

"This is untrue!" Patel protested through clenched teeth as he looked briefly into the eyes of the two agents before glaring over at the photo of Mutasi and him smiling at Wimbledon.

"Are you for certain, Mr. Patel?" probed one of the Pakistani analyst retrieving a retractable pen from his inner jacket pocket and scribbling something down on a yellow stenopad. Patel watched them intensely, slowly pondering how he would deal with Mutasi.

"Sir, you mentioned that you had little to do with the intel on your company, Calvary Ltd being sent to Wikileaks?" pressed the other agent.

"Absolutely not! I had nothing to do with this. Forgive me, but this is the first time that I am aware of this information," Patel answered only to notice a brief silence as one of the agents continued to scribble something down on the notepad.

"Mr. Patel, you must be aware that the government of Pakistanistan has fully supported the endeavors of your company."

Patel nodded.

"You and your company have provided jobs for our people and aided in the technological boost in our economy."

"Yes...this I realize," Patel replied somberly.

"Good. Then you also must know that your relationship with Mr. Mutasi has caused a bit of strain on how the government of Pakistanistan views you."

"But I have no relationship with Mutasi!"

"Then how do you explain the friendly photograph of you and he situated on the bookshelf to the left."

His dark eyes drifted slightly yet he remained un-phased by the agents' line of questioning. Patel waited a beat before replying coldly.

"We were two men enjoying a tennis match."

"Are you for certain?" probed the agent. "You would have us believe that there was no business between the two of you whatsoever?"

"None that would jeopardize the image of myself, my company or my country." Patel answered directly noticing the quick exchange of glances between the two agents.

"Very well then," added the agent as the other stopped writing, clicked the retractable pen once and closed his stenopad. As the two men rose to their feet to prepare to leave, Patel asked them the questions that had bore a hole in his soul throughout the impromptu interrogation.

"Who is Khalid Mutasi really? What is his birth name and who does he work for?"

Smirking slyly the Pakistani agent who had asked all of the questions faced Patel as if he'd been anticipating the moment.

"The birth name of Khalid Mutasi is Qasim Kaled. He is a western journalist and asset to the CIA."

Sinking into his chair Patel acted just as the intelligence officers thought he would. He was crushed. Their job was complete – they had nothing else to do there. Walking out of the office the two agents bid Patel farewell and left the building. Grabbing a hidden bottle of vodka out of left bottom drawer of his desk, he opened it and took a long hard gulp before grabbing his Android phone and making a call. Within seconds a husky male voice answered the phone.

"You have deceived me!" snarled Patel in Urdu before letting the man on the other end get a word in edgewise.

"Never!" the man replied nervously.

"Then how did this journalist infiltrate the company, hmm? You and Masoud were sent to Dubai with specific orders to eradicate the westerner and the mole," he growled before taking another gulp of the vodka and grabbing a handkerchief out of his blazer to wipe his brow.

"I know of no journalist."

"Well he knows of me and you!"

"What will you have me do?" the man pressed.

"Find him! Destroy him!" Patel said with urgency.

""It shall be done. Where is he now?"

"Who?"

"Mutasi?"

"That is for you to find out!" Patel growled before ending the call abruptly and finishing what was left of the vodka. The last thing he needed was any of his on-goings to be posted on WikiLeaks. Up until this point he had been quite successful in making strategic alliances within the Libyan government without consulting with Calvary Ltd's CEO, and respected businessman Faisal Rashid in Dubai. The less Rashid knew, the better. Patel's plan was to eventually take over all satellite operations of Calvary and buy out Rashid. He'd already done it with the U.S. office in Texas. But he could only do that with the right political alliances. Financing energy deals in the West was exactly what Patel did for emerging infrastructure companies in Pakistanistan, parts of Africa, and Syria. With the assistance of the Libyan government Patel could make Calvary Ltd. the only company to boost energy infrastructure in Lebanon, and Morocco. Sure, Rashid had the support of most of the Arabian Peninsula but he couldn't penetrate North Africa like Patel. He just didn't have the business acumen to do so.

There was no way Patel would let anyone stand in his way. Once he eradicated the journalist, things would go back to business as usual – at least that's what he preferred to believe.

Tossing his Android in the open desk drawer, Patel quickly hid the vodka bottle and tossed a mint in his mouth before opening the door and walking out of his office.

"Vashtie?" he said to his secretary in English.

"Sir?"

"Book me a flight to Dubai. I need to be there tomorrow first thing. I'd like to make sure that business out of the Dubai office is handled effectively."

"For how long will you require accommodations, Mr. Patel?" she asked gently, her hazel eyes, fringed with lush black lashes, flickered slightly as she awaited his response.

"Two weeks. No need to tell Mr. Rashid. My visit should come to him as a surprise," he said as he began to walk past her desk, but stopped in mid stride. "Oh and Vashtie?"

"Yes, Mr. Patel?"

"Book me at the Burj!"

"Your usual suite at the Burj al Arab,sir?" Vashtie asked as Patel gave a quick nod before walking towards the elevators. He pressed the button and as the doors opened, immediately stepped into the open car available.

Just as the elevator car doors closed, Vashtie quickly got up from her desk, and walked into Patel's office closing the door behind her. When things were secure, she pulled out her mobile phone and checked in with her source. Within moments of speed dialing her source, a British accented voice answered the call.

"Vashtie Bizri? How are you, love?"

"No time for formalities, Dawud."

"I sense the urgency in your voice. What's the latest?"

"Patel has plans to leave for Dubai tonight," she began in a hurried whisper as she shuffled through the papers on Patel's desk. Meanwhile, as Patel reached the 3rd floor he remembered that he'd left his Android phone and keycard to the Karachi Golf Club in his desk drawer. He had to go back up. Exiting the elevator on the 3rd floor, his timing was impeccable as he hopped on the car adjacent to the descending one that he was initially on. He only had two floors to go before he was back up in the suite.

Scrambling through the papers on Patel's desk, Vashtie continued to divulge all of the particulars of the planned trip to CIA asset Dawud El-Hashem.

"Wonder why he's going to Dubai," Dawud asked.

"Something went awry. Yesterday I believe. I overheard him yelling at someone in Urdu," she said not realizing that the elevator doors were beginning to open and Patel had already begun to step out into the suite.

"I'm searching for the bug I'd put in here earlier, so I can transcribe what was said" she said, stopping short of what she was doing and pulling the phone away from her ear. As her eyes scanned the walls of the office, it finally dawned on her that she could hear Patel's voice. It travelled quite well through the walls. He must have been just outside. Panicking, she quickly ended her call to Dawud, promising to check back in later. Opening his desk drawer she noticed Patel's cellphone and keycard which she abruptly picked up and carried with her. Opening the door to exit Patel's office in a deft move she tucked her mobile phone just under her ample breasts in her bra and quickly slid back into her seat behind her desk. Luckily, he was too immersed in a conversation with a fellow associate in the elevator to notice her come out of his office. Placing the Android phone and key card at the top left corner of her desk, Vashtie placed her headset on and pretended to be ending a call.

Her heart beat was heavy in her chest as her breath quickened and mouth went dry. She let out a brief sigh of relief as he began to walk towards her.

"I was just about to call you, sir" she began smoothly.

"Oh? And why is that?" he said coldly.

"You left your mobile at your desk. When I called I heard it ring," she offered as she intentionally knocked her pen off of the desk and seductively leaned over, revealing a bit of her cleavage, just to pick it up. Distracted temporarily by the slight temptation she afforded him, Patel's demeanor changed. Temptation was great and Vashtie was beautiful, but he knew there was business at hand. Placing the pen on the computer keyboard, Vashtie covered her low cut blouse with her shawl before allowing her eyes to meet with his. Trying hard to hide the hunger, Patel nodded once at her before giving a bit of praise.

"You are always right on schedule, Vashtie" was the best that he could come up with given the bulge quickly rising in his pants and the lump forming in his throat. Grabbing the phone and keycard, he glanced quickly at her once more before making his way towards the elevator doors.

"You can reach me on my mobile, should you need me," he said with his back towards the woman as he slipped through the elevator doors.

3

The Al Mahary Radisson Blu Hotel was just another hotel in the weary eyes of Agent Jones. While its central location afforded him the easiest access to Tripoli that he needed, Jones had gotten quite accustomed to the opulence of Dubai and felt that this was indeed a step down. He would've much rather stayed at the regal Rixos Al Nasir, the enthralling Plasma Hotel or even the luxurious Corinthia Hotel - at least there he would've had the five star accommodations and mesmerizing, sea breeze Mediterranean views that he'd grown so accustomed to seeing these past few weeks in the middle east. If he was lucky, maybe he'd be able to take in the hypnotic lilac and blood orange infused sunsets that Libya was known for from his hotel room if and only if his room faced the sea. While a walk on beach that blanketed the Mediterranean was exactly what he needed, he knew that he was there for business only, not to indulge in the pleasantries that Tripoli had readily available for the taking.

Exiting the car and walking into the hotel lobby, he noticed one of Tripoli's finest exotic pleasantries standing behind the concierge desk. Everything about her was poised and perfect and if he could find two more just like her then his business in Libya might not be so bad. He could tell that she was of the upper class due to her westernized style and lack of a hijab. Adorned in gold bracelets that were 24 karats each, and two 3 carat diamond rings set on platinum bands Jones found himself wondering why she was working there. Her jewelry alone said volumes about her economic background, unless of course, she was a *nikah al mutah* - a temporary wife - maybe to a wealthy businessman or to a member of the aristocracy. He knew that he'd better not make his opinions vocal, lest he might suffer severe consequences. Certain things you just didn't discuss in the Arab World, especially when the phrase *nikah al mutah* could've easily been equated with calling this woman a whore. Unlike in America, the word "whore" was never to be used to reference a woman at any time in Libya. Unless, of course that woman was being accused of adultery and even then, Libya was one of the more liberal countries in the Arab world. Jones was no fool and he knew enough about Islamic teaching to know that a temporary marriage is forbidden in Islam.

Stepping up to the concierge desk, Jones quickly went into his cover for the mission.

"Good afternoon, sir. Welcome to the Al-Mahary Radisson Blu," she said warmly making eye contact with him.

"Good afternoon," Jones replied in the British accent he'd feigned at the airport 30 minutes before.

"How may I help you?" she asked eagerly.

"I have a reservation under the name Qadir," Jones began. He watched as the woman's delicate, tan hands and perfectly manicured red finger nails, keyed in his name on her computer. She paused a bit while waiting for the reservation to come up.

"Ah yes. Mr. Ali Qadir?" she asked.

"Actually it's Ahmed Qadir," Jones corrected her.

"Yes sir. My apologies I misread your name," she said her face flushed red after she misread his name. After offering an apology she made eye contact quickly before requesting Jones' credit card, passport and visa. Obliging her request he handed everything over and waited patiently as she cross checked his identification with what was listed on the reservation. Grabbing the card key to his room, she handed the credit card, passport, visa and hotel room key to Jones.

"Mr. Qadir, your card was already on file and everything checks out. You are in suite 332, Ali will escort you up. Is there anything else that I can assist you with?"

"I think you have handled everything perfectly....Noor," he said quickly scanning the concierge's name badge. Startled she looked up at him briefly before remembering that she was wearing a badge. Smiling warmly she motioned to the lithe man wearing a red and gold uniform who quickly lifted Jones' suitcase and placed it on a luggage rack.

"I hope you enjoy your stay here, Mr. Qadir."

"I will. Thank you."

"Now, if you will kindly follow Ali he will escort your up to your suite," Noor nodded once at Ali and bashfully smiled at Jones who thanked her once more and gave a quick wink before following Ali into the elevator.

Silence filled the elevator on the way up to the suite. Jones looked once or twice at the bellboy only to receive an awkward smile and nod. Initially, he thought that the whole setup wasn't right but the doors to the third floor opened, he quickly shrugged off the feeling. At a glance he couldn't tell if the bellboy was Libyan, Indian or Middle Eastern. All he knew is that he didn't like the vibe that he got from him.

"Right this way, Mr. Qadir," he offered stepping out of the elevator with the luggage rack and waiting for Jones to step out. As soon as he was out of the elevator, the bell boy walked several paces ahead before stopping abruptly at suite 332.

"Your card, sir?" the bell boy requested as Jones fumbled around for the key card. Once he found it he handed it to him. Inserting the card, then removing it, the bell boy opened the door to reveal one of the more impressive Junior Suites. Stepping into the suite, Jones was immersed in a breathtaking, panoramic view of the Mediterranean Sea. The mod décor was more visually stunning than he had anticipated. Everything in the suite was actually...doable.

As the bell boy placed Jones' suitcase in the front room closet, he asked if there was anything else required. Shaking his head, Jones swiftly reached into his pants pocket and handed the guy a ten dinars note which featured a picture of the leader of the resistance martyr Omar Almokhtar. The bell boy thanked him and left the room.

Ironically, just as Jones was settling into his hotel suite, Izzie was directly above him making a phone call to Cunningham from her mobile.

"Ms. Musabi!" he answered promptly.

"Sir, Jones is…"

"In the building? Yes, I know."

"But I…I don't understand. I thought you wanted me to call and check in with you upon his arrival."

"And, it seems you have done just that," Cunningham replied sounding a bit preoccupied.

"What will you have me do then?" Izzie pressed vying for a bit more direction from Cunningham. Snickering at her question, Cunningham waited a beat before answering.

"You can wait in your room for further instructions from Dawud El-Hashem or you can go up to the 15th floor in about an hour, have a drink, take in the view and meet him face-to-face. Then you will be briefed on what is yet to come."

Izzie did not like Cunningham's tone. Something was a bit off about it. Nonetheless, the last thing that she felt like doing was sitting around in her hotel suite waiting. Since it seemed like she had time to spare, it came as no surprise to Cunningham that she would choose the latter.

As a matter-of-fact, that was exactly what he wanted her to do. Cunningham needed to hear firsthand from El-Hashem himself how he knew Izzie. Their little chat in the airport had made his guard go up and he felt that he didn't know all that there was to know about Izzie Musabi. That was a bit of a problem, because now he wasn't sure whose team she was playing for.

Feigning a calm demeanor Izzie told Cunningham she'd be on the 15th floor in an hour and ended the call. Tossing the phone on the sofa in her suite, Izzie quickly removed the coral hijab, threw it on the chair and walked over to the closet where she'd placed her backpack. Opening it, she removed what looked to be a pocket-sized, leather bound copy of the Quran. As she unzipped the leather exterior, she removed a color photograph of her and an older man on a yacht with the name "Carcharias" inscribed in gold on the side. Staring at the picture briefly, she shook her head after turning it over to review the text on the back which had the word "informant/double," scribbled on the back. Taking a deep breath, she quickly zipped the book back up and placed it neatly in her bag before making her way to the bathroom, and starting the water for a shower.

As she removed the two hair pins that were holding her hair in place from her hair, she walked out into the bedroom suite, grabbed the remote and turned on the tv. Flipping through a few channels, she stopped when she found MTV and turned up the volume significantly. If she was to have an hour to herself, she wanted to enjoy it as best as possible. Disrobing quickly, she entered the shower hoping to drain her thoughts away.

Settling into his hotel room, Jones couldn't help but take in the panoramic view of the Mediterranean from his window. Simply put, it was stunning, calming, soothing – it was everything he never imagined it could be. Instinct urged him to open the balcony door, but he chose against it – opting to grab a file folder out of his briefcase instead. He needed to get to the bottom of things and he knew he didn't have much time. He needed to know who or what the Pakistani connection was. Somehow, someway Libya held the key to him finding out the truth.

Fumbling through the file he wasn't entirely sure of exactly what he was looking for. All he knew was there had to be some connection – something that he may have overlooked. Scanning emails, maps and copies of handwritten notes from various members of Calvary Oil, Jones could not manage to find anything. Just as he was about to give up, his mobile rang. Unsure of who it could be, Jones thought it best to play it safe.

"Ahmed Qadir," he answered in his feigned British accent.

"Jones...the line is secure," a familiar voice replied.

"Can't be too sure, Cunningham."

"True. Look, in approximately 45 minutes you'll be meeting the asset. His name is El-Hashem....Dawud El-Hashem."

"Ok." Jones said apprehensively – his British accent waned completely.

"Is there anything I should know about him?" he pressed.

"Nothing comes to mind. El-Hashem will fill you in when you meet him."

"What does he look like? And...where will we meet?"

Cunningham noticed that Jones was full of questions. Although Jones was always a bit precocious for an agent, Cunningham still didn't feel like answering 99 questions about the assignment.

"Jones?"

"Sir?"

"You know how these things go. The asset will come to you. So there is nothing to tell about him except that you will know him when you see him."

"Ok."

"In 45 minutes you are to go up to the Business Lounge on the 15th floor. Order two drinks. A vodka martini for yourself, and a vodka tonic for El-Hashem."

"Anything else?"

"You are to request that the vodka tonic be made with the best top shelf vodka in the bar, and the vodka martini be made with Albanian Raki."

"Albanian Raki?"

"Yes. It is the smoothest vodka out. It has a much better taste than all others. This will be a good talking point for you when it comes to El-Hashem."

"And why is that?"

"Because, my friend, he is a vodka connoisseur."

"I see."

"When he asks you why Albanian Raki, your response should be because it's smoother."

"Got it."

"Good. So get up to the lounge within the hour. He will be expecting you."

Ending the call after those words, Cunningham pulled out a Cohiba Lanceros cigar from his desk and took in the pre draw taste. He didn't want to light it just yet. Instead he played with the platinum cigarette lighter on his desk - flicking it on and off – immersed in his thoughts. Although he was stuck in Abu Dhabi, he had a feeling that things were about to get heated in Tripoli – all the key players were in place – so all he had to do was watch where the chips would fall.

Buzzing his secretary, he requested an update on - Izzie's background. Ever since that conversation he had with her earlier he was eager to know how she knew El-Hashem. As the secretary walked into his office, he noticed that in a short time span she managed to collect quite a bit of information on Izzie. Handing him a fully stacked accordion file folder, the secretary stood quietly as Cunningham looked at the contents apprehensively before motioning for her to leave. Randomly pulling out a sealed manila envelope with Izzie's name scribbled across the front, he was hardly prepared for what lay inside.

4

Karachi, Pakistan
Karachi Golf Club
20 Minutes Later, Same Day

The journalist, Khalid Mutasi (aka Qasim Kaled) who had outted Mustafa Patel sat nervously at the bar in the clubhouse fumbling with a toothpick in his right hand and a near empty tumbler glass in his left. Swallowing a huge gulp of grain liquor, the man motioned for the bartender to bring him another.

Something was troubling him – so much so that disdain was etched heavily all over his face. Truth is, Mutasi had been hiding out on the grounds of the golf club for a week now, hoping and praying that he would not run into Mustafa Patel. Although he'd been advised by the feds to leave the country, Mutasi decided against it and instead squandered his flight money on alcohol and Russian prostitutes instead.

He'd played the conversation that he had with the feds over and over in his mind like a broken record. He recalled every word to perfection. And while he had traded the secrets to Patel's success in exchange for flight money, he still felt he had an ace in the hole with the information that he hadn't given up. It was the single most damaging piece of information that had the potential to destroy the Calvary Empire. And he wanted to be paid for this information or at the very least be paid to keep quiet about it.

Hoping for the latter, he decided to cut his losses on the flight ticket and wait for an even bigger pay out from none other than Patel himself. He figured that with his knowledge of such damaging information, he could demand upward $2 million dollars to be placed in a Cayman Islands bank account under one of his aliases or maybe even his real name. By now, he figured that Patel already knew his true identity, so what did he have to lose?

The stakes were high in the blackmail game that Mutasi was playing but with him being a professional grifter by trade, he thought he had this one in the bag. If that were true why was his gut telling him to abandon the plan?

As the bartender topped up his drink, he stared in a daze at the Islamic art piece hanging on the wall. It was done in Arabic calligraphy and looked much like the sultan's tughra from the Ottoman days. So immersed was he in the art, that he hardly noticed his mark walk in and take a seat at the table behind him. Just as he paid off his tab with the bartender, he slowly turned around and unintentionally their eyes met. Patel looked at Mutasi with flaring nostrils and a raised eyebrow, before the man pumped out his chest and boldly walked over and took a seat at the table. As the waiter brought over his drink, Patel sipped slowly as he glared angrily at Mutasi. A smirk soon came to his lips as he set the drink back on the table and finally broke the awkward silence.

"Khalid Mutasi...what brings you to my table?" Patel said sarcastically. The undertones of his voice seethed with a hint of passive aggression that could turn deadly at any moment.

"Why Mustafa? You know why I am here?" Mutasi replied condescendingly.

"Do I? Please...enlighten me," Patel said coldly, as he snapped up the wine glass that sat in front of him, and took a hearty gulp.

"Mustafa my friend I have a proposition for you," Mutasi began trying to sound as calm as possible only to see Patel laugh coldly in his face.

"You...Have a proposition for me? Come now, Khalid. Just this morning two lieutenants from the spy agency came to my office to question me about you, and how you posted damaging information about my company on Wikileaks. Not to mention how you led the governments of three countries believe that my humble endeavors through Calvary Oil were a criminal act, a terrorist threat and an enemy of the state. What could you possibly have that I would want?" he sneered – his aggression rising as hot beads of sweat began trickling from his brow. As Patel wiped the sweat with a nearby napkin, Mutasi thought it a good idea to take a different approach.

"Information, Patel. Damaging information."

"Ah, more damaging information, Mutasi, hmm? This, my friend I do not believe."

"Then it is your loss for I was prepared to negotiate," Mutasi said as he stood up and began to walk away from the table. Curious as to what he may have up his sleeve, Patel waited a beat before beckoning for Mutasi to come back and motioning for him to have a seat. Things were going just as Mutasi had planned.

"Why have you called me back?" he pressed.

"Curiosity, my friend," Patel said sounding like the devil himself.

Nodding his head, Mutasi retrieved a small digital camera out of his jacket pocket and turned it on. Before saying anything further he directed Patel's attention to one of the photos on the LCD screen of the camera.

"This is you, accepting payments from Mikail Davidoff, a known Ukranian sex trafficker, who pilfers models from the popular Haut Monde Model Management Company as call girls to the rich, is it not? And here...this is you checking in at the Langham Hotel in London nearly two weeks ago with a very modelesque yet underage companion. Ah, and this is one of my personal favorites. This is you engaged in deviant sexual behavior with said companion. And here you are paying for the service," Mutasi said to Patel in Arabic. Looking at all of the photos carefully, Patel wanted to deny but knew that there was no way out of this situation. When Mutasi had shown him five additional photos, all close-ups of the illicit transactions with him front and center in the picture, Patel realized that he was in a now win situation. If he denied it, then Mutasi would plaster the photos all over the media in s smear campaign within minutes.

However, if he acknowledged it, he'd have to fork over a handsome amount of money to keep the man silent. The only way to get out of the present situation was to eradicate the Mutasi problem. Patel had already placed a call a reliable hit man but the only problem was that the hit man was in Dubai. Inhaling deeply and reaching for his box of Djarum Blacks out of his jacket pocket, he pulled one out and offered it to Mutasi. Eagerly taking the smoke, Mutasi was ready to negotiate. Lighting both his and Mutasi's cigarette, Patel asked the question that Mutasi had been waiting for.

"What is the price to make all of this go away?"

"I am a very fair man, Mustafa and an prepared to make this little blemish disappear for a mere $2 million USD," Mutasi said noticing Patel's poker face glaring coldly without blinking. $2 million was an obscene amount of money for information to disappear. But Patel continued to play along.

"When?"

"Within the hour."

"Impossible."

"Oh?"

"I do not keep that sort of money in Karachi."

"We both know otherwise, no?" Mutasi asked before taking a long drag from his cigarette and exhaling through his nose. With eyes asquint he leaned in towards Patel.

"I know you have access to it."

"And how do you know this?"

"Do you not think I have access to your bank records? Hmm?" Mutasi pressed snidely taking a quick drag from his cigarette and leaning back in his chair.

"I see," Patel offered nonchalantly.

"I will expect you to wire the funds to this account in the Caymen Islands," Mutasi said as he slid a business card over to Patel with three, handwritten lines scrawled across the back.

Patel looked snidely at the information on the card before returning his gaze up to Mutasi whose overconfidence made him want choke him on sight. Picking the card up from the table and slipping it into his inner jacket pocket, Patel gave Mutasi a quick nod before returning his attention to his glass of wine.

"It shall be done," Patel said trying to ignore the lump in his throat.

"Within the hour?"

"Of course. As you wish."

"Inshallah, my friend. As always, it is a pleasure doing business with you." Mutasi said as he stood up and walked casually away from the table. He could hardly believe how easy that went. He decided to play a few rounds of golf to celebrate. As soon as Mutasi was out of sight, Patel placed a call.

"Change of plans!" he whispered in Urdu. "I will take care of the problem."

"Sir?" said the rugged male voice on the other end.

"I will take care of Mutasi. You will wait for my call," Patel said coldly as he ended the call and placed yet another to his assistant. The phone rang a full three times before she answered.

"Mr. Patel?" she answered. "I have booked your flight to Dubai as you requested. You'll depart at…"

"Vashtie," he interrupted. "Postpone the flight."

"But sir?" she objected.

"I feel that it is time you took on a special assignment."

"Sir?"

"You cannot be so naïve to believe that I hired you without knowing your history," he said calmly, removing the business card that Mutasi had given him and examining it closely. He noticed the uncomfortable silence that came from Vashtie's end.

"So you know that I was a…"

"You must understand that it was your work as a professional exterminator for the Americans which inclined me to hire you."

"What is it that you require of me, Mr. Patel?" Vashtie said this time trading her professional secretarial tone for a more sultry and no nonsense tone. She realized now that Patel had always had the upper hand in this game. But she had a few secrets of her own that he still didn't know about.

"In one hour, funds will be transferred to a Cayman Island account for Qasim Kaled. You will need to arrive at the Karachi Golf Club within the next 20 minutes and go to tee up on the green. I will arrange for you to relieve his caddy."

"I will need someone to dispose of the body," Vashtie whispered. She was, after all, still at the Calvary office. Discretion was essential.

"Upon arrival, come to the club house for further instructions."

"As you wish, sir."

"Oh and Vashtie…I need this to be swift and clean. It cannot be traced back to me."

"With all due respect Mr. Patel, I am a professional" Vashtie said just prior to Patel snickering and ending the call.

Placing the mobile back in her desk drawer, Vashtie grabbed her purse and looked in her wallet for the spare syringe filled with 1080 – the undetectable poison sodium fluoroacetate - she usually kept in there for emergency purposes. Luckily it was still there. Adjusting her hijab and grabbing the mobile out of the drawer, Vashtie told one of the other assistants that she was leaving for the day and took a cab over to the golf club.

<u>5</u>

As-shahab Port
Tripoli, Libya
Sametime

Dawud El-Hashem was almost undistinguishable from the other men at Tripoli's As-shahab Port. Unlike the average billionaire, El-Hashem didn't seem to have a problem with the obscurity. He was on assignment and fully immersed in a makeshift war game and he was loving every minute of it. As it was, he had 10 minutes to get to the 15th floor of the Radisson Blu, and while it was only one sea road away, time was completely of the essence. El-Hashem had to meet with both Izzie Musabi and J. Jones separately of course, yet all within a 20 minute window of time. As he prepared to deboard his yacht, Carcharias, he had the staff on his yacht unload his customized, chrome-wrapped, Can-Am Spyder Roadster on the sea road along the port. After giving detailed instructions to his staff, El-Hashem hopped on his roadster and sped over to the Radisson Blu.

Within 5 minutes he approached the valet drop off, turned off the ignition and hopped off the bike exchanging his keys for a valet number as he walked into the front doors of the Radisson Blu. He smiled warmly at the beautiful concierge and walked casually over to the elevators. He hadn't been waiting 30 seconds before a car going up opened its doors. Stepping into the elevator he pressed the button for floor 15 and enjoyed the ride.

Meanwhile, Izzie had just walked into the Business Lounge and awkwardly took a seat at a table in the north corner overlooking the sea. As the waiter came over to her table, she ordered Arabian coffee no cream and a pastry. As she stared out of the window she hardly noticed El-Hashem slide into a seat at her table.

"Hello, love," he said taking her hand in his.

"Dawud...it has been a long time," Izzie said as she quickly withdrew her hand from his.

"That it has, my dear. Cunningham tells that you are working with the Americans now?"

"I am a fed, yes."

"That's too bad, love. Life could have been much easier for you had you stayed with me."

"You mean, played with you, Dawud? I'm not interested in your games."

Feigning surprise, Dawud looked briefly at Izzie, before waiving the waiter over to the table and requesting his signature vodka martini.

"Right. Listen darling, there's much work for you to do. First, you are to tail Jones everywhere he goes. Next, you are to do what I need you to do."

"Or?"

"Or, what, love?"

"Is there a consequence to me doing things my way, Dawud?" Izzie pressed getting a bit emotional.

"Life is full of consequences, Izzie. You know that just as well as I. So, off you go, then."

"What?...Why?"

"Jones will be here momentarily, love," Dawud said nonchalantly as the waiter placed both his vodka martini, her coffee and pastry on the table. He gave the waiter a quick nod of thanks before focusing his attention back on her.

"Right. I guess I'll…" she said suddenly losing her appetite.

"Just wait for my call, love? Ok?"

Izzie felt as if Dawud was blowing her off. She didn't want to believe that he was still sour over her ending their affair years ago, but she couldn't help but to wonder. She knew that billionaire like him had their own moral code, and Dawud was not the sort of man who wouldn't make up his own moral code along the way. She hated that he knew of her life as a Cannes call girl who worked for Haut Monde Model Management before she turned CIA asset. She was sure that she'd kept she kept Cunningham and the agency off the scent, but with El-Hashem now in the mix, she wasn't entirely sure what information about her past was out there. What if Cunningham found out everything – the prostitution, the lies, and even the fact that her real name wasn't even Izzie Musabi. What if he found out that her twin sister was a hired assassin? What if, what if, what if? The things that ran through her mind were endless. And she didn't know if she could count on El-Hashem not to betray her. Just before she exited the business lounge she requested that her coffee and pastry be delivered to her room. Izzie had a lot on her mind and thought it would be a good idea to take the stairs instead of wait for the elevator. Just as the door to the stairway closed behind her, the elevator doors to the car immediately adjacent to the stairs flew open and J. Jones walked out.

Smoothing out the wrinkle in his sports jacket, Jones casually walked in to the business lounge and waited to be seated. It wasn't long before a waiter escorted him to a table in the center of the lounge. Taking in the breathtaking view, Jones opted to go against Cunningham's instructions and ordered a Gentleman Jack and Coke on the rocks. Reviewing the menu while waiting for his drink, he caught El-

Hashem approach and slide into the seat opposite him at the small table.

"Dawud El-Hashem, I presume?" Jones said in his posh British accent.

"You presume correct," El-Hashem replied in an equally posh accent.

"Good to finally meet you," Jones said smoothly returning his gaze back to the menu and thanking the waiter as he brought over his drink. Taking a long sip of the smooth brew, a smirk formed on his lips before he commanded El-Hashem's attention with four poignant words.

"What's your poison, Hashem?"

"Vodka Martini. Stirred. And the name is El-Hashem, Mr. Jones."

"Ah, yes. Pardon the miscommunication."

"Not to worry, my friend. It happens quite frequently when I travel to the states."

Jones nodded before taking a quick sip from his Jack and Coke then requested that the waiter bring a vodka martini to the table.

"Is Belvedere ok, sir?" the waiter asked.

"No. I think Albanian Raki is the wiser."

"Right away, sir" the waiter replied before scurrying off to the bar.

"Albanian Raki? I must say, Mr. Jones you've got quite the penchant for exceptional vodka."

"I try, Mr. El-Hashem."

"Right. So let's drop the formalities, for now. You are to address me as Dawud or simply by my surname. The choice is yours, Jones."

"Done."

"It is okay to call you Jones, is it not? Although when Cunningham briefed me, I found myself wondering what the J., in your first name stood for."

Jones glanced at El-Hashem condescendingly. He would have expected a handler like him to know this already. Jones was beginning to believe that El-Hashem was hiding his true motives.

"The J. stands for Jeronimo but while I'm in Tripoli the name is Ahmed Qadir."

"Jeronimo was the name of a fearsome warrior. How intriguing. But you wish for me to refer to you as Ahmed Qadir?" El-Hashem pressed for an answer just after thanking the waiter for his drink and taking a lengthy gulp from it.

"Cheers!" he said after a sigh of satisfaction, then returned his attention to Jones.

"Look...Jones...err...Qadir. I am here to help you; to give you vital instructions, and even permit you to use any of my resources during your stay here in Tripoli."

"Understood."

"As Cunningham gives me details I give them to you and provide you with all necessary tools you may need. Be it business,

financial or intercontinental – my resources are...how shall I say...
limitless . But of course you fully understand this."

"Yes, I do. " Jones said not entirely sure what El-Hashem was
getting at.

"Good. I am told that you need an in at Calvary Oil, is that
right?"

"Yes."

"And you also need a way to get to the dictator directly, no?"

"This is true, yes."

"Alright. Tonight a car will take you to my yacht for a dinner
party that the dictator will be attending. You will be one of guests.
One of my best escorts will be provided to you."

"An escort?"

"Ah yes. You in the west call them social companions. Look,
mate, I thought you knew - I own shares in several modeling agencies.
Haut Monde, Legacy, Affinity and Du Monde. The biggest agencies in
the world."

"Never heard of them."

"C'est une honte!"

"Pardon?"

"You, my friend, should brush up on your French. C'est une
honte is, 'What a shame!' If ever you're to fit in as a foreign dignitary or
friend of mine – you need at the very least to be fluent in French,
Arabic and Portuegese. I can arrange for the escort to give you the best
in private lessons if you like." El-Hashem said with a raised eyebrow to

which Jones smirked slyly. He just might enjoy this mission after all. Taking another hearty sip from his martini, El-Hashem steered the conversation back to business.

"Work hard, play hard, Jones, no? I think so. In three hours a car will take you to the Ashahab Port. Look for the boat Carcharias. It cannot be missed. A member of my staff will escort you to my office where I'll be waiting."

"Ok. But how will I meet his majesty if I am only in Libya on business as an oilman?"

"Tonight, you will not be a mere oilman. Tonight you are the People's Majlis of Adonai Isle."

"Adonai Isle?"

"It is one of the islands that I own in the Maldives."

"How far is it from Vagaru Island?"

"Ah..I see that you are familiar with the Maldives, then?"

Jones nodded once.

"Well Adonai Isle is roughly 70 kilometers south of Vagaru in the Addu Atoll. I like to believe that Adonai is the pièce de résistance of The Maldives. Lucky for me, his majesty agrees."

"I see."

Jones still wasn't entirely sure what tricks El-Hashem had up his sleeve but he sat and continued listening intently all the same. Taking a huge gulp from the vodka martini El-Hashem looked at Jones carefully before placing the glass back in front of him.

"Do you have any questions for me, Jones?"

"No El-Hashem, I do not."

"Very well then. I will see you in three hours on Carcharias."

"Looking forward to it," Jones replied watching cautiously as El-Hashem stood up and left the lounge. Once he was in the elevator and out of earshot of Jones, El-Hashem made a call to a member of his staff.

"Is it finished?"

"No sir," replied his Pakistanistani outfitter.

"The reason?"

"It seems as if the target has left her room."

"Interesting. I'd given her express instructions to wait for my call."

"What will you have me do, sir?"

El-Hashem thought about this for a moment before making his demands.

"You are to go into her suite and wait for her. She can't possibly be too far."

"And then?"

"And then you are to carry out the order as planned. Keep it clean...neat...it must look like an accident or a suicide even. Report back to Carcharias within the hour," El-Hashem said snidely before hanging up the phone and stepping off of the elevator into the hotel lobby.

6

Karachi Golf Club
Karachi, Pakistanistan
15 minutes later...

Sauntering into the lobby of the clubhouse, Vashti Bizri commanded everyone's attention. Her voluptuous frame, dewy-golden-olive skin, hypnotic hazel-green eyes, and crimson-stained, plush, pouty lips were just the vision that made many a businessman in the clubhouse utterly breathless. She was the walking embodiment of everything they missed at home.

As she scanned the room, she immediately saw that Patel was seated at a table near the bar. Sashaying over and sitting down, Vashti noticed that Patel was on edge in he seemed somehow bewitched by her intoxicating, carnal beauty that not even her dupatta scarf could obscure. Patel could only imagine how lush her hair was beneath the scarf and he took quiet reverie in undressing her with his eyes. While he knew that this was a business meeting, he could not ignore how she acquiesced raw sensuality.

"Vashti, you are a vision!" he proclaimed as she lowered her eyes bashfully and smiled.

"Thank you, Mr. Patel. But if you would be so kind, please tell me where can I find the mark?" She was all business and Patel knew it. He'd dealt with her kind before and expected the services to come at a hefty price.

"Ah yes, the whereabouts of the mark? I'd failed to give you that information," Patel began as he finished the last of his wine, never once taking his eyes off of her. He couldn't stop thinking about how earlier she briefly revealed a hint of her supple femininity to him in the office. He wiped his lips and brow with a napkin before sliding the once full glass back onto the table. He was aroused and didn't care if she knew it.

"The mark is playing a round of golf, my dear," he said nodding his head over towards the door once only to settle his gaze back on her.

"On which side of the course, sir?"

"North."

"Of course...of course. He is not expecting my company is he?"

"No. Not at all. You my dear, will be a great surprise. I happen to know that he has rented a small villa on the premises."

"I see, and by chance, would you know the number of the villa?"

"I believe it is number 3."

"Number 3? Noted." Vashti replied after pondering the many ways that she could eradicate the mark. It wasn't long before she settled on one.

"As requested, I cancelled your travel arrangements to Dubai, Mr. Patel," she said noticing another patron walk by. Leaning in closer to the table, Vashti lowered her voice to a near whisper.

"If you want the mark completely eradicated, I may need a little more time."

"How much time, my dear?"

"Three hours."

"And in this three hour window, you can guarantee extermination?"

"Indeed. Mr. Patel, you must realize that this sort of work is rarely done for free."

"But of course, my dear Vashti. Please name your price?"

"For complete annihilation of the target...it is fixed at $10,000 USD."

"And?"

"A visa and a one way ticket to Tripoli."

"Libya or Lebanon?"

"Libya."

"Quite, reasonable. Consider it done," Patel said as he scratched his temple and ordered another glass of wine for himself. He'd offered to get one for Vashti but she kindly declined.

"Mr. Patel, I will need half of the fee up front," she said as she seductively ran the side of her thumb across her moist, crimson lips.

Patel sat in awe of how Vashti worked. Her no-nonsense, hit-woman demeanor made him want her even more. Getting $10,000 was an easy feat. Getting $5,000 was easier. He'd decided at that very moment that he would not only meet her needs, he'd exceed them and end up having her all to himself after she eradicated the Mutasi problem. Staring at her intensely he signaled for the waiter to come to the table. Once there he scribbled a written request down for the waiter to fulfill and smoothly removed a crisp, $50 bill from his pocket and handed it to him.

"Right away, sir" the waiter proclaimed before being stopped in mid-stride by Patel's heavy grip.

"How long?" he whispered to the young man.

"No more than 7 minutes, sir" the waiter replied to which Patel nodded once and released his grip.

Vashti sat in silence, waiting patiently for Patel to when she'd collect her fee. Taking in her curves from head to waist, Patel took yet another sip of his wine before entertaining her inquisitive eyes.

"You will have your $5,000 USD momentarily, I have sent the help to retrieve it."

"And what of the other half, visa and flight ticket?"

"You will have this once I have proof that the problem has been eliminated."

"What is your definition of proof, Mr. Patel?" Vashti pressed. "After all, you said to keep things clean."

"And so I did. But I would like to know that he has been eradicated."

Before Vashti could object, Patel continued.

"Mutasi has an iPhone with extended video capabilities."

"Are you suggesting that I film it?"

"But of course. How else am I to know that the service has been completed?"

Vashti was coming to realize that Patel was much more heartless than she could've ever anticipated.

"I see. Well, since my image – full or partial – will be connected to your burden of proof, you will need to pay $5,000 more."

"And for $5,000 more I will require the entire affair filmed from start to finish."

"Start to finish?"

"Yes. Start-to-finish."

"But the iPhone is not equipped to capture three hours of footage," she objected.

"You are a clever girl, Vashtie. I'm sure you'll find a way."

"The price just went up! I will need $7,500 USD within the hour then!"

"And, my dear, you shall have it."

As the conversation came to a close, the waiter honored Patel's request and brought over yet another glass of wine as well as a small envelope that held $5,000 USD. After handing the envelope to Patel, the waiter quickly disappeared into the crowd of patrons leaving Patel alone with Vashtie once more. Examing the contents, Patel slid the envelope over to Vashtie who quickly tucked it into her purse.

"Aren't you going to count it?"

"No need." Vashtie replied.

After confirming the number of the villa once more, she stood up and made her way out of the clubhouse, leaving Patel to drown his misery in yet another glass of wine.

Sashaying over to the nearest caddy, Vashtie managed to find out exactly where Mutasi was playing as well as where his villa was situated. Her intial plan was to make him suffer slowly but since time was of the essence, she'd make it quick. She wasn't entirely sure how to bait him. If she stayed on the green, chances were that he'd equate their meeting chance instead of circumstance. He'd want to take here to dinner - get a little more acquainted. Vashtie had no time for dating shenanigans so she decided to pay the caddy to tell Mutasi that something of great urgency had been delivered to his villa. The caddy was not to tell him who the message came from. Mutasi would more than likely think that it was his payoff from Patel. And that's just what Vashtie wanted him to think.

As she sauntered into his villa, she quickly undressed leaving on nothing but a string of pearls around her neck and 4.5" red bottomed heels. She used her dupatta as a veil and draped it across her body seductively, so when Mutasi came in all he'd see was a silhouette of her curves in the dimly lit room.

She hadn't been sitting in the villa for more than 15 minutes when Mutasi came in searching for his special delivery. When he caught sight of her dew, glistening skin against the Bordeaux chaisse lounge he approached her carnally.

"And who might you be?" Mutasi asked staring at every inch of her curves.

"I am your special delivery," she replied, her cold and calculating nature was masked by her seductive charm.

Mutasi looked her up and down twice before walking past her. There was something strangely familiar about her.

"That cannot be," he said.

"How do you figure, sir?" Vashtie pressed.

"Because I'd never order the likes of you!" he snarled looking over at her with disgust. Vashtie grew angry and her face flushed red.

"The...likes...of...me?" she questioned.

"Uhm...hmm. A dusky bitch like you could never please me," Mutasi replied coldly. "You've made a mistake coming here, my dear."

Anger consumed Vashtie. She'd never been dismissed quite like that. She was humiliated, and enraged. For this alone, Mutasi would pay. Instead of using the syringe like she'd planned, she opted to use her pearl handled, 44 magnum semiautomatic. She wanted to see the fear in his eyes when she took his life.

Still fully nude, she pulled out her magnum with the silencer already attached. Mutasi was muttering insults with his back towards her. Calmly, Vashtie aimed the semi-automatic at him.

"Forgive me...I must have the wrong villa," she said coldly. Mutasi was no fool and after hearing the cold tone of her voice, he realized where he'd recognized her and knew it was a set up. With his snub-nosed 9mm discreetly in his hand, he turned around and prepared to shoot. But to his chagrin, Vashtie shot him twice hitting him in the shoulder and stomach before he could even squeeze the trigger. She walked over as he slid to the floor from the impact of the shot. Hovering over him while in the nude gave her the most unbelievable high that she hadn't felt since the first time she killed someone. Struggling to speak, Mutasi coughed and blood seeped slowly out of his mouth. Seeing that he still clutched the gun in his left hand, Vashtie kicked it away before squatting seductively by his side.

"Shhh...shhh...It will be over soon," she said soothingly.

Coughing twice more, Mutasi squirmed in pain as a puddle of blood quickly began to cover the floor. Muttering something else, Vashtie bent down to hear what he was trying to say.

"Dusky…bitch! I recognize you. You were a hooker in Cannes. Worked for him… two…years…ago…It was you…*you*!" he said struggling to breathe with lips trembling and tears streaming from his bloodshot eyes from the pain.

Vashtie methodically put the nose of her 44 up against his temple and pulled the trigger. Silence consumed the room as she stood up, walked over to the chaise lounge and put her clothes back on. Recalling that Patel needed proof, once she was fully dressed she sashayed over to Mutasi's dead corpse and snapped a picture with her iPhone.

"How's that for a dusky bitch?" she snarled as she stared down at Mutasi's lifeless body. Careful not to step in the blood, she casually walked out while making a call to Patel.

"It is finished," she said closing the door to the villa behind her when he answered the phone.

"Are you certain?" he probed.

"But of course."

"According to plan?"

"Yes. Mr. Patel, I have told you several times that I am a professional."

"And this I see."

"I can meet you at once to collect the balance."

"Vashtie, I did not expect you to complete the task so quickly. So I have not had the chance to make the arrangements for your visa or flight out of Karachi," Patel said hoping to coax her into stopping by his personal villa so that he could indulge in her sexually. An awkward silence came from Vashti's end. After all, that was not part of the deal. It was now time for the trump card to be served.

"Mr. Patel, you have 15 minutes to make the financial transaction with me."

"Or what, my dear?"

"Or I will finish the work that Mutasi started and lodge two bullets in your head!"

Normally Patel would've called her bluff, but the ice cold tone in her voice told him to think otherwise.

"14 minutes, now" Vashtie said coldly before ending the call.

Patel sat motionlessly still at the table in the clubhouse. He didn't completely trust Vashtie but at the same time since the work was complete, he knew he had to pay up or risk being exposed to the media. Motioning for the waiter once more, he quickly wrote a dollar amount on the napkin and urged the waiter to get it wired to him quickly. Within 15 minutes, the waiter had returned with a cash stuffed envelope. Waiving him away, Patel called Vashtie and requested that she meet him where she left him at the table in the clubhouse.

It didn't take long for Vashtie to arrive. When she found that he did not get the visa or the flight ticket, she was beyond words. She knew that within hours the police would be crawling around the golf course. The job that she'd done for Patel was sloppy and she knew it. So she had no other recourse but to get out of town quickly. Not wanting to hear his small talk, she grabbed the envelope off of the table as soon as she saw it, promised to send him a photo message within the hour, gave him a quick nod and left. Instantly, Patel had a feeling that she was holding something back. Things just didn't feel right.

Within 30 minutes of her leaving he'd received a photo message from an unknown mobile number. After it uploaded he realized that his gut feeling about her was right. Noticing how messy she did the job made him furious. Not only did she make it look like an apparent homicide, she also used a gun. After a little research the authorities would undoubtedly name him as a prime suspect.

"Bitch!" he growled as he grabbed a napkin and wiped his mouth. His head began to spin as he speed dialed his enforcer in Dubai. Within moments the man answered.

"There is a problem," he began in hushed Urdu.

"Sir? Is it the one you wanted me to handle earlier?" the enforcer asked.

"No!" he snapped. "It is much bigger."

"What will you have me do?"

"How quickly can you get to Dubai International?"

"Within minutes, sir?"

"Good. Then I will have the company jet prepared for your departure."

"Where am I to go?"

"Libya. My problem will be in Tripoli in 6 ½ hours, my jet will have you there in 5. Are you near a computer?"

"Yes."

"Good. I am sending you a photo of the problem from my iPad," Patel waited a beat after clicking send.

"Have you received it?" There was a long pause before he answered.

"Yes, I have it," the enforcer replied. "This is the problem?" he pressed.

"Yes. You are to make her go away."

"What method did you have in mind?"

Patel thought for a moment before answering.

"It should look like a domestic dispute. She is to look like the immoral woman...who got caught."

"I see."

"In the states it could easily look like a robbery but in Tripoli it must look more domestically provoked."

"This problem of yours is quite attractive."

"But she is completely messy."

"Sir?"

"Nevermind. Just make sure that you eradicated all possibility of her survival. Your fee plus 15% will be awaiting you on the jet."

"Yes sir. It shall be done."

Disconnecting the call, Patel phoned headquarters and requested the jet prepare for take off and sent a private car to pick up his enforcer. No one, no matter how intriguing, would make him the fall guy. He thought Vashtie understood that.

Patel knew after he made the arrangements for his enforcer that he too had to get out of Karachi. So after he chartered the company jet out of Dubai, he called his local driver to take him to Lahore where he could get a train ride into Delhi, India and blend into the local scene for a while. Eventually he'd make his way over to his estate in Marrakech, Morocco. No one would ever think to look for him there. Not to mention with Vashtie scheduled to be eliminated in Tripoli, he'd have the perfect alibi should he need it.

Instantly he paid his tab in cash and slipped into the car, ordering his driver to get to Lahore the fastest way possible. He figured that Mutasi's body would be found within 2-3 hours, which was just enough time for him to make a swift passage to India via Lahore.

<u>7</u>

Hailing the first cab she saw in front of the golf course, Vashtie slipped into it and barked for the driver to take her to the airport. It had finally set in that she botched the hit and she had to get out of the country quick. Fumbling through the contacts on her phone she stopped when she came to El-Hashem's name. Usually she was not one to cash in on favors but she was in a jam. Pushing his name the call connected within two rings.

"El-Hashem here."

"Dawud?"

"Vashtie?"

"Yes. Yes. I could really use your help."

"Slow down, love. What is it? What's going on?"

"I need a visa and a flight to Tripoli. Can you help me with that?" she whispered.

"Sure, if you tell me what's going on."

"No time. Can you help me or not?" Dawud waited a beat. He could hear fear in Vashtie's voice which is something he'd never heard before.

"Okay, love. I take it you need these things now?"

"Yes please."

"The lady says please. Hmmm....you must be in trouble. One moment, love."

After a few moments of silence and hard keystrokes, Dawud returned to the call.

"Okay love, you're on the next Emirates flight out. Leaves in 30 minutes. I have you travelling under the alias Meera Ramadan as an analyst for Hashem Properties."

"Meera? Like the actress?"

"You catch on quick, love!"

"I try. Thank you, Dawud. I will explain as soon as I get there."

"Of course you will, love. My driver will be picking you up. We will talk then."

As he ended the call, El-Hashem, thought of a better way to eradicate the Izzie Musabi problem. He'd have her very own flesh blood, Vashtie – her sister- take her out. After all, Vashtie owed him for the flight, and Izzie's life would be the perfect payment.

Dawud El-Hashem was one of the few people in the world who could: make things happen at will and make people disappear without a trace of evidence. He was what non profit, non partisan activists for global change would consider an individual of undue influence or a member of the billionaire oligarchy who benefitted financially from global crises. Was he more powerful than the president of any given nation? But of course! Because he funded nations and was a prime financial resource for global banks. He wasn't just a mere businessman, he was a walking , talking global empire – a superpower who always got what he wanted.

Just like anyone else in the world, El-Hashem had an agenda behind everything that he did. So, when he opened an invitation to both Izzie and Jones to be guests on his yacht, the motive wasn't simply to provide instructions to junior agents. It was more or less to stir the proverbial pot of mayhem and mischief and if all went according to plan, murder. He knew that Jones was in the dark about Izzie tailing him on this mission. He also knew Izzis secret past was something that she didn't want senior agent Cunningham or Jones to know about. Furthermore, he knew that by coming to the rescue of Izzie's evil twin sister Vashtie, that things could easily get interesting at the planned soiree.

Vashtie was essential in the elimination of Izzie and it helped that Vashtie utterly despised her twin. When the two saw each other, feelings of betrayal and rage would inevitably take over and El-Hashem would finally be rid of the liability known as Ishtar Musabi. It's not that he wanted to kill her – it's just that in his world human life was expendable. And when he learned how dedicated Izzie was to her work as a federal agent, she instantly became a liability to him. He just couldn't take the chance of her connecting the dots between him, Calvary Oil and the dictator of Libya. Not to mention, Izzie's curiosity could inevitably lead her to the truth behind his company, Carrollton Investments, being a mere front for the underground network of illegal arms smuggling in North Africa.

He could tell from his conversation with Izzie in the business lounge earlier that she was eager to prove herself. It was only a matter of time before she discovered the truth. As he thought about these things in his office, he quickly picked a brown dossier off of his desk and placed it in a safe just below his mahogany credenza. Before he could close the door to the safe agent Jones walked in.

"Ah… Jones. Or should I say Qadir?" he began a bit startled.

"Jones is fine, El-Hashem. Quite an impressive boat you have here," Jones replied, not using his feigned British accent.

"Ah yes! Carcharias is the most exquisite. You, my friend, certainly are dress the part," El-Hashem said waiving away the crew member who brought Jones to the office. Meanwhile Jones glanced over at the file in the half opened safe before engaging in conversation with El-Hashem.

"Uh…yes. You mentioned that el Presidente would be aboard and that I would…"

"Yes, you will be introduced as the shah of my Island in the Maldives. But of course, Jones. I remember."

Jones stood rigid, unsure of what to expect from El-Hashem. As the man walked back to his desk, Jones studied his moves, wishing he could discern what El-Hashem stood to gain from his posing as a shah.

"La Isla Adonai. The Isle of Adonai, no? Mr. Jones, there is very little I can forget when it comes to business. Please, join me on deck for a drink," El-Hashem said as he motioned for Jones to follow him up the stairs.

Lingering behind El-Hashem, Jones quickly glanced back at the partially opened safe before quickening his stride to meet up with his gracious host.

"Would you like a cigar, Mr. Jones?" asked a sensuous woman – impeccably dressed in a fitted, customized tuxedo, halter mini dress. Her deep brown eyes and plush lips intrigued Jones while the sultry back seam of her stockings invited him to learn more.

"I see you have a bit of a weakness for Capricorn," El-Hashem snickered as he pulled two Romeo y Julieta tubos from the platinum tray that she was holding and thrust one into Jones' hand.

"Capricorn?" he finally said.

"Uhm-hmm. She is one of my assistants," El-Hashem replied as he flicked his gold lighter twice to light Jones' cigar before his own.

"How many do you have?"

"Assistants or Capricorns?"

Laughing, both El-Hashem and Jones walked over to the bar where they were promptly served.

"Mojitos?" Jones said after a quick sip.

"Seemed appropriate given the weather, ambiance and of course... the women. Now you inquired about Capricorn. She, my friend, is one of a kind. There is no other quite like her."

"Understood, but I was inquiring about the number of assistants that you have."

Taking a few puffs from his cigar, El-Hashem placed his drink on the tray of a passing butler before addressing Jones.

"Aboard Cacharias, I have 10. In the field...thousands. All the best businessmen do."

"But of course. So tell me, Dawud...what am I really here for?"

El-Hashem waited a beat before addressing Jones. He was beginning to sense that the junior agent was not as dumb as he looked. Taking a much needed puff from his cigar, El-Hashem glanced over at one of his assistants whose gaze revealed problem.

"You are in Libya to investigate a..."

"This is not what I mean. Why am I aboard your ship?" Jones pressed.

"You are my guest, Agent Jones. So relax, and enjoy the affair. Now if you'll excuse me, there is something that requires my immediate attention," El-Hashem said as he swiftly made his way over to his assistant.

Meanwhile, Jones found that his curiosity was consuming him. He had to know what was in that safe. So when he thought no one was looking, he slipped away from the upper deck and went back downstairs to El-Hashem's office. Since people were finding their way aboard the ship, no one noticed that he was not on deck. Walking into El-Hashem's office, he closed the door behind him and headed right for the safe. The safe was ajar, so his plight was easy. Pulling out a half hidden folder, he couldn't help but to open it. Just as he began to read the contents, he heard footsteps clank swiftly down the stairs. Whoever it could be was heading his way. Quickly, closing the door to the safe he clutched the folder against his chest and hid in the tight space between the bookcase and the wall. His heart beat quickened as he watched through the reflection in the credenza glass who entered the office.

The creak of the door squealed briefly as a small framed woman entered the room and closed the door behind her. He could hear her rustle through the papers on El-Hashem's desk before her cellphone rang.

"Yes?" she answered impatiently still rustling through the papers. Jones wondered what the woman was looking for and hoped she wouldn't come his way.

"Look man...I'm on it!" she said ...her voice seemed vaguely familiar to Jones.

Opening up a few desk drawers it was apparent that the woman could not find what she was looking for. Sighing heavily on the phone, the woman paused before replying.

"Agent Cunningham, I've got everything under control. I've tracked Jones to the yacht party and will proceed as planned."

"Cunningham!" Jones thought. In that moment things began to make sense and he knew that the woman had to be Izzie. The one thing he didn't know was what plan she and Cunningham had cooked up for him.

Just as she ended the call, the door to the office opened abruptly.

"Ah, there you are love. I've been looking all over for you." Stunned Izzie stood rigid looking at El-Hashem.

"I got lost...looking for the restroom," she offered.

"Oh, of course you did, love. No harm in that."

"No. I supposed you're right. Speaking of the restroom, where is it?" she asked calmly.

"Not to worry, love. You won't be needing it."

Suddenly two men took hold of both her arms and dragged her out of the office. Jones could hear her protest and then there was silence.

"Get her out of here. That shot will wear off in 20 minutes."

"Where should we put her, boss?"

"Stow her somewhere – the mechanical room, perhaps."

"Right, boss!"

"And lock up the office. We wouldn't want anyone else to get lost down here, now would we?"

"Right away, boss!"

Within seconds Jones heard the deadbolt lock from outside of the office. Stepping out from behind the bookcase, Jones took a deep breath before opening the folder. The first page was a list of names.

"Vashti Bizri, Mustafa Patel, Ishtar Musabi..."

It was some sort of weird triad where those three individuals were linked by a single thread known as Calvary Oil. The next page was a ledger of financial transactions. It looked like money transfers to Calvary Oil Pakistan. At first, Jones thought that they could be stocks, but then he realized that was not possible. The subsequent pages had all kinds of handwriting and diagrams. Three words were circled.

"Keifer Arms and WikiLeaks?" Jones muttered.

Some of the handwriting, Jones simply couldn't make out. He took a few quick photographs with his mini cam and quickly rifled through the remaining contents of the folder. He stopped short when he came to a photo of Izzie and then a separate photo of a woman who looked like Izzie, but on the back "Vashti Bizri...twin of Musabi" was scrawled.

Stunned for the moment Jones struggled with how to process the information and connect the dots. One thing was for certain, he knew that he couldn't trust El-Hashem, Cunningham or Izzie. Right now, he was on his own and El-Hashem was more dangerous than he'd ever imagined.

"The best ally is a conquered enemy."

-Mustafa Patel

www.agfielder.net
(author/series creator)

www.domestika.org/portfolios/alfonso_rosso
(illustrator)

Get the latest intel on J. Jones at his official website:

www.i-am-j-jones.net

Illustrated By: Alfonso Rosso

www.ingramcontent.com/pod-product-compliance
Lightning Source LLC
Chambersburg PA
CBHW070534130626
46555CB00003B/1416